The Leprechaun's Gold

By Pamela Duncan Edwards

Illustrated by Henry Cole

Katherine Tegen Books
An Imprint of HarperCollins*Publishers*

L ong ago, before even your great-great-grandfather was born, there lived in a small village in Ireland a man known to all as Old Pat.

Old Pat was a harpist, and a good one at that. Many a wedding was made the merrier by Old Pat's harp.

In the same village dwelled Young Tom. Tom had learned his own harp playing from Pat's teaching. But now, Tom thought himself a better harpist than Old Pat. He was much given to boasting and bragging and charging the villagers great amounts of silver for his skills.

Old Pat was humble and willing to play his music for free for those he knew had not the means to pay.

"Foolish old man," scoffed Young Tom. "What use is a gift if not to make you rich."

Old Pat replied, "I am rich in friends, and that is enough."

It is to be supposed that life would have continued along its way for Old Pat and Young Tom had they not seen the announcement:

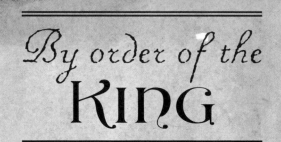

By order of the
KING

Harping Contest

To Choose

The Finest Harpist

In Ireland

At The Royal Palace

All May Enter

"To be known as the best harpist in Ireland would be an honor indeed," said Old Pat.

"Don't waste your time, old man," sneered Tom. "It's a young man like myself they'll be wanting."

But Pat shook his head and gathered his few meager possessions for the journey.

Aha! thought Young Tom. If we travel together, he's sure to offer me a bite of his food. That would save me a penny or two.

And so it was that on this night the two sat together by their fire of twigs. They were footsore and weary from walking the many miles toward the Royal Palace.

As he listened to Pat practicing for the contest, a sudden thought flashed through Young Tom's mind: I could lose to this ridiculous old man.

So, as Old Pat turned his head for a second, the wicked boy quickly snapped a string on Pat's harp and pushed his own spare string deep inside his bag.

"I'm sorry for your trouble," he said to Old Pat. "But I have no string to lend you, for I might need it myself."

Old Pat sighed. He had no money to buy a new string. The harping contest was as good as lost.

Then, suddenly through the darkness, came a cry. "Help!"
The two men shivered, for they knew tales of tricks played
on poor travelers by villain leprechauns.

"Surely 'tis the little people that's after us," whispered
Young Tom.

But as the voice rose to a wail, Old Pat's kindness of heart proved stronger than his fear of leprechaun tricks.

"We must find out who's in trouble," he cried to Tom.

"Not I," declared Young Tom. "I'll have nothing to do with it. I'll not take the risk of missing the contest." He turned his back to the voice and covered his ears.

On shaking legs, Old Pat walked toward the sound of the voice.

In a clearing, he saw a tiny man with his foot down a rabbit hole.

"Help me, sir!" cried the little man. "I took off my shoes to rest my feet, and a rabbit has taken hold of my big toe. Help me!"

From deep in the burrow came the shrill laugh of the rabbit.

"Let go, you rogue," the little man yelled down the hole. "I'll have you for dinner, you pesky bag of flea-ridden fur!"

I'll soon fix that scoundrel, thought Old Pat. He bent down and barked piercingly as a fox might in the night.

The rabbit let out a scream of fright, and out popped the little man's toe.

"Thank you," cried the leprechaun, for a leprechaun he was!

"Come," said Pat, trying not to laugh, for a funnier sight he thought never to see. "I've not much to offer, but what I have you're welcome to share."

Old Pat led the leprechaun back to the fire.

"I see your fellow traveler has up and gone," said the leprechaun. "A brave fellow indeed he proved to be. But I thank you kindly for your help. I'd like to repay you."

"I'll be needing no payment," answered Old Pat. He picked up his harp and began to play a soft tune to soothe the little man.

"You play well," said the leprechaun. "But I'm thinking your harp is not in a good way."

"I have a broken string," answered Old Pat sadly. "I'm on my way to the harping contest at the Royal Palace. But I'll not win now. I have no money to buy a new string."

"Ah!" declared the leprechaun sharply. "So it's the gold you'll be wanting!"

"No indeed!" cried Old Pat, mighty alarmed. He knew terrible things happened to those who searched for crocks of leprechaun gold.

"Ah, but yes! I think it's so!" answered the leprechaun firmly.

Suddenly Old Pat's eyes would not stop from closing. With a sigh, he fell asleep. The leprechaun blew a silvery note on his whistle. Out of the forest came a band of little men, each carrying a bag.

"He wants the gold," said the leprechaun as he told the tale of Old Pat. "You know what to do!"

The little men nodded solemnly as they clicked open their bags.

When Old Pat awakened the next morning, he looked around in fright. But the leprechaun was gone.

"It's a lucky escape I've had," cried Old Pat, as he picked up his harp case and set off for the Royal Palace.

As Old Pat reached the courtyard, Young Tom took the stage, looking mighty pleased and confident. He began to play a sweet tune but, as if bewitched, the strings on his harp began to break. One by one, they twanged and twitched and twirled in the air, until all lay dangling.

Young Tom gazed at his harp in horror. But then he knew. "Leprechauns!" he muttered, as he hung his head and shuffled from the stage.

Now it was Old Pat's turn. With sadness in his heart, the old man reached for his harp. Then his eyes widened. For there, inside his bag, lay a glittering golden harp.

"The leprechaun's gold!" gasped Old Pat.

He lifted the golden harp and began to play. He played the merriest music ever heard, so wonderful that the wind itself stopped to listen. A wild tune it was, which filled the people's hearts with joy and their lips with laughter.

As the magic seized their feet, the people began to dance. Soon the courtyard was filled with a dancing, singing, laughing crowd.

The other harpists knew now that this was Pat's day and danced along with the people. Even Young Tom, who had learned a hard lesson, found generosity growing in his heart.

When the final note faded away, the king rose from his throne and beckoned to Pat.

"Old man," said the king, "the prize is yours. Never have I heard such music. From now on you will play always for me and my people. You are awarded the title Royal Harpist of Ireland."

From the nearby forest

came the tinkling sound

of a little leprechaun laughing.

There are sixteen four-leaf clovers in this book.
Can you find them all?

To my friends Margaret Lane
and Joan Darnell, with love
—P.D.E.

To Barb Sizemore,
a wonderful teacher, with thanks
—H.C.

The Leprechaun's Gold
Text copyright © 2004 by Pamela Duncan Edwards
Illustrations copyright © 2004 by Henry Cole
Manufactured in China.

Library of Congress Cataloging-in-Publication Data
Edwards, Pamela Duncan.
The leprechaun's gold / by Pamela Duncan Edwards ; illustrated by Henry Cole. — 1st ed.
    p.   cm.
Summary: A leprechaun intervenes when a greedy young harpist sabotages a royal contest.
ISBN-10: 0-06-623974-5 — ISBN-10: 0-06-623975-3 (lib. bdg.)
ISBN-10: 0-06-443878-3 (pbk.)
ISBN-13: 978-0-06-623974-3 — ISBN-13: 978-0-06-623975-0 (lib. bdg.)
ISBN-13: 978-0-06-443878-0 (pbk.)
[1. Leprechauns—Fiction. 2. Greed—Fiction. 3. Harp—Fiction. 4. Ireland—Fiction.]
I. Cole, Henry, ill. II. Title.
PZ7.E26365 Le 2004   2002003150
[E]—dc21

Typography by Elynn Cohen ❖